Tale of the Poisonous Yuck Bugs

Aaron Reynolds

Illustrated by Pete Whitehead

Zonderkidz

Zonderkidz®

The children's group of Zondervan

www.zonderkidz.com

Tale of the Poisonous Yuck-Bugs
ISBN: 0-310-70955-5
Copyright © 2005 by Willow Creek Association

Requests for information should be addressed to:
Zonderkidz, Grand Rapids, Michigan 49530

Library of Congress Cataloging-in-Publication Data

Reynolds, Aaron, 1970-
   Tale of the poisonous yuck-bugs : based on Proverbs 12:18 / by Aaron
Reynolds ; illustrated by Peter Whitehead.
      p. cm.
   ISBN 0-310-70955-5 (hardcover)
   1. Insects--Juvenile poetry. 2. Kindness--Juvenile poetry. 3.
Conduct of life--Juvenile poetry. 4. Children's poetry, American. I.
Whitehead, Peter. II. Title.
   PS3618.E965T35 2005
   811'.6--dc22
                          2004012261

Design: Merit Alderink
Art Direction: Michelle Lenger & Merit Alderink

Illustrations used in this book were created digitally using Photoshop.
The body text for this book is set in Triplex Bold and WhoaNelly.

Printed in China
05 06 07 08 09/SCC/5 4 3 2 1

Thoughtless words cut like a sword.

BUT THE TONGUE OF WISE PEOPLE BRINGS HEALING.

— Proverbs 12:18

ISLAND OF GAK

On the Island of Gak,
in the Gakkle-back Sea,
way up on the branch of a boingo-leaf tree,
live two bugs that are scary—as scary can be.

These bugs are the yuck-bugs. There are two, as I've said.
One yuck-bug has blue spots—the other has red.
If you were to see them, two creatures so small,
you'd say to yourself,

"THEY AREN'T SCARY AT ALL!"

But they're poisonous, these yuck-bugs.

They're toxic, they reek.

For their poison is found in the words that they speak.

"You jerkulous jerk!" one will shout from their tree.

"If you're hearing me now then you're dumber than me!"

Then the other will shout, "No one's ugly as you!"
to whoever's around, they don't really care who.

And the creatures nearby all get sick when they hear them
So the creatures of Gak try not to get near them.

And so that's how life was, with them yucking that way,
shouting poisonous words. UNTiL, ONE DaY...

They were up in their tree.
They were eating away
on a boingo tree leaf
that they'd picked fresh that day.

RIP!

They were there chomping hungrily,
chew after chew,
when the one with blue spots
ripped the leaf right in two.

"You twerpulous twerp!" said the red-spotted one.
"You've ruined my lunch. Now my meal is all done.
I'll only eat leaves that are un-ripped, you see.

YOU ARE CLUMSY AND DUMB
AND YOU STINK UP THE TREE!"

There's a rule among yuck-bugs that's never been broken.
It's a really big rule, though it's kind of unspoken.
"Yuck-bugs never talk to other yuck-bugs that way."
Well, this unbroken rule had been broken that day.

"I shouldn't have said that. I didn't mean to."
But the words had slipped out as such words sometimes do,
and the poisonous words did their poisonous trick,
and the blue-spotted yuck-bug began to get sick.

He opened his mouth
and yelled through his pain,
"You skunkulous goof!

IS THERE SLUDGE IN YOUR BRAIN?

You dare break the rule
and use yuck-words on me?
Well, I can use yuck-words on you,
watch and see!"

The red-spotted yuck-bug
started to sway
for the word "skunkulous"
has extra poison they say.

And his foul cousin's words
did their foul nasty trick,
and the red-spotted yuck-bug
began to get sick.

Backwards and forwards the words flew this way
on that terrible poisonous-word-flinging day.
And the more poisonous yuck-words the two yuck-bugs threw,
the sicker and sicker the two yuck-bugs grew.

At last, they were lying there,
very near dead
from the poisonous words
THAT THE OTHER HAD SAID.

And our yuck-bug story might be over now
if an odd twist of fate hadn't changed things somehow.
For landing that moment, way up at tree-tip
was a very rare bug on a very long trip.

The watch-what-you-utterfly is a rare bug indeed,
and this rare utterfly eats a rare kind of seed
that is found far away on the Mountain of Meer.
So the utterfly flies to it twice every year.

But such a long flight, well, it's tiring at best,
so the watch-what-you-utterfly took a short rest.
And so, spreading her wings,
she touched down there and then
on the branch
on the tree

THAT THE YUCK-BUGS LIVED IN.

As the yuck-bugs lay lying there,

dying there still,

from the poisonous words

that they'd used with such skill,

that rare utterfly

uttered something quite rare:

Well, the blue-spotted yuck-bug felt something un-yuck
inside of him, deep, where the yuck-words had stuck.
"And that blue one," the utterfly uttered. "Look there!
SUch GORGEOUS RED SPOTS ON THaT OTHeR BUG THERE."

Then the red-spotted yuck-bug
felt an un-yucky feeling
as his wounds from the poisonous
words started healing.

See, the watch-what-you-utterfly has a great power.

Some say that it comes from the Meer Mountain flower.

Others say that it comes from the nectar she drinks.

But the truth is, it comes from the words that she speaks.

For the un-yucky stuff in the words that she'll say
makes the yuck from the yucky words all go away.
And that's what the yuck-bugs were feeling right now.
THEIR INSIDES WERE UN-YUCKING AND HEALING SOMEHOW!

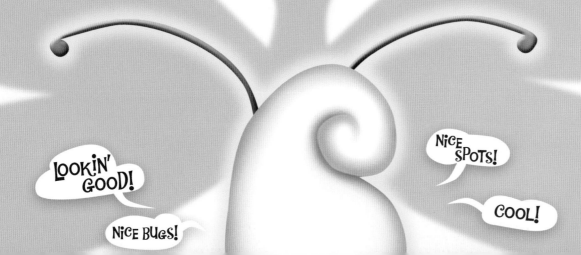

LOOKIN' GOOD!

NICE SPOTS!

COOL!

NICE BUGS!

"Well, I've had my rest now, but I really must say
That meeting you insects has brightened my day."
And the watch-what-you-utterfly fluttered away.
And those two little yuck-bugs who'd been almost dead

WERE STANDING UP TALL, FEELING STRONG NOW INSTEAD.

Just how they were saved, they still haven't guessed
about the utterfly bug who had stopped for a rest.

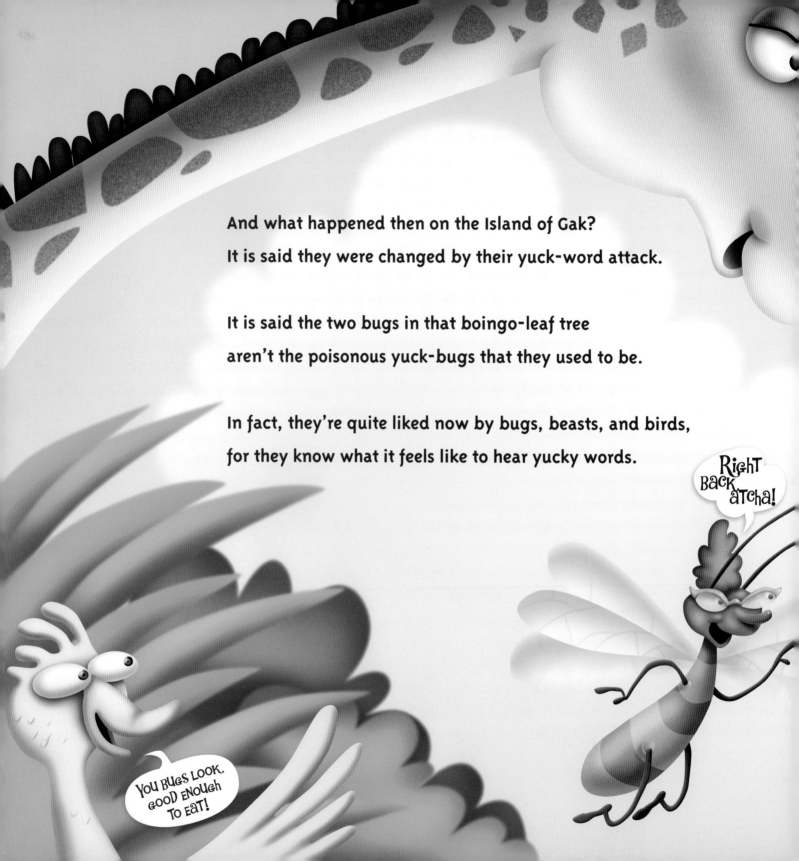

And what happened then on the Island of Gak?
It is said they were changed by their yuck-word attack.

It is said the two bugs in that boingo-leaf tree
aren't the poisonous yuck-bugs that they used to be.

In fact, they're quite liked now by bugs, beasts, and birds,
for they know what it feels like to hear yucky words.

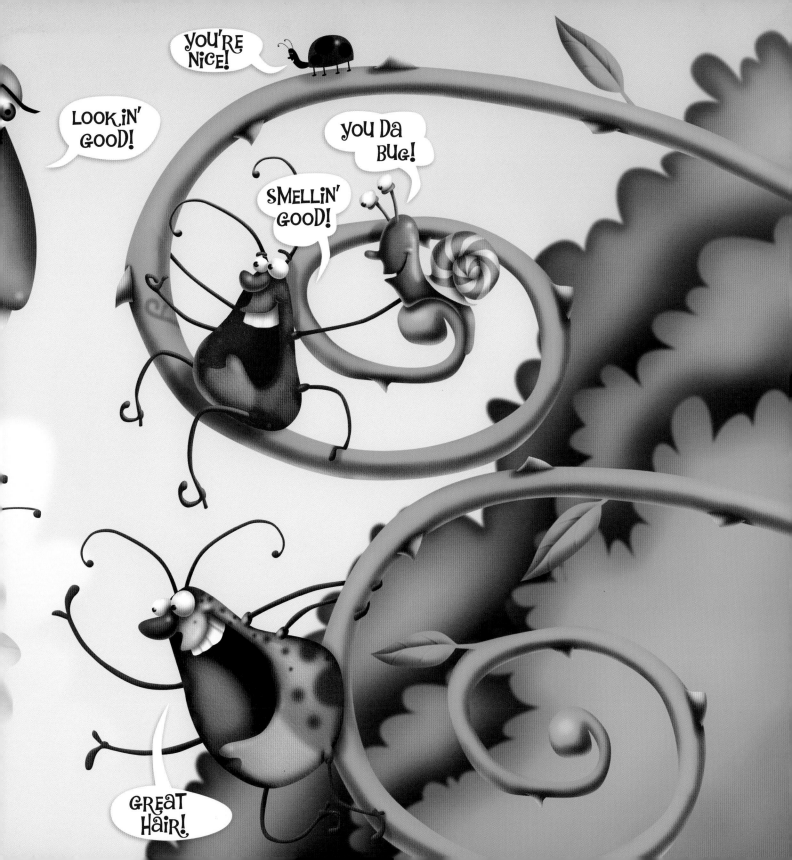

Ouch! That Stings!

Ever wonder why it bugs you so much when somebody says something mean to you? Even a little put-down can sting. Okay, so you're not going to keel over dead when somebody tells you that you stink at baseball or that your clothes don't match. But the truth is: words can hurt. Luckily, the opposite is true, too.

Metamorphosis Challenge

Try this. Next time you feel yucky words creeping out of your mouth, do the opposite. Think of something nice to say about the other person—and then say it. It doesn't have to be any big thing, and you don't have to lie or make something up. How about, "Awesome job in the kickball game today!" or "Hey, cool jacket!"

While yucky words really hurt, encouraging words—even little things—have an amazing power to make people feel better.

This isn't a freshly hatched idea. God's been saying it for ages. Check it out for yourself in Proverbs 12:18. You'll see that wise people know the healing power of nice words.

Yucky words, on the other hand—they're just a dead end.